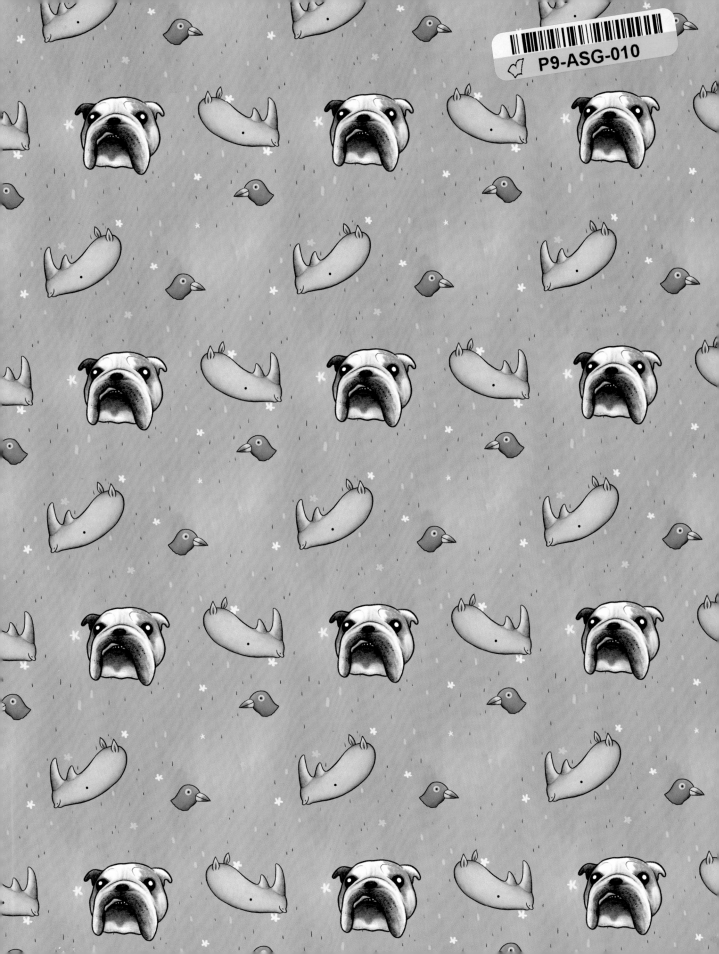

You may know me as a shark, but I'm a rhinoceros, too.

Lulu and I have a lot in common. When I was young, I was different from the other kids around me. I was on a mission. I told anyone who would listen—and anyone who *wouldn't*—that I was born to build something big. Even when everyone doubted me, I believed in myself. Sometimes that was really hard, especially when things weren't going my way. Those times when I was questioning myself, when I was about to lose hope, one person never wavered.

Like Lulu, I have a tickbird.

My mom has been my partner, my cheerleader, and—as Lulu helped me realize— my tickbird, for my whole life. When I told her who I was and what I was going to do, she believed in me without question, no matter how crazy the plan might have seemed. I know who I am, and I *am* who I am, because of my tickbird, my mom.

Lulu's also got big plans, and she believes in herself even when others don't. I hope she inspires you the way she inspired me, and helps you find your tickbird, too.

- *Daymond John*

Lulu Is A Rhinoceros

Author: Jason Flom with Allison Flom
Illustrator: Sophie Corrigan
Publisher/Editor: Michael Hermann

Wicked Cow Studios

President/CEO: Michael Hermann
Chief Content Officer: Adam Hirsch
Chief of Staff: Matt Russo
Creative Director/Book Design: Samantha Merley

Third Edition
Printed in Canada

Library of Congress Control Number 2018903538
ISBN Number 978-0-692-07098-7

Lulu
is a Rhinoceros

By Jason Flom
with Allison Flom

Illustrated by
Sophie Corrigan

What I am *not* is a bulldog.
In fact, I am not a dog at all.

Can you guess what I am?

I'm a
RHINOCEROS!

In my heart, I have thick gray rhino skin!
But what I really have is soft, fuzzy fur.

In my mind I have a tail that
whips and twirls! But what I see is a
little nub that wiggles when I'm happy.

But the only thing
I don't have yet,
that I really,
really want...

Is my rhino HORN.

Hi, I'm a rhinoceros

Eeeeek!

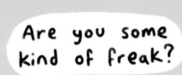
I'm a rhinoceros

Are you some kind of freak?

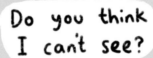
I'm a rhinoceros!

Do you think I can't see?

I. AM. A. RHINOCEROS!

You don't look like one to me!

If I only had my horn, they would finally see the REAL me!

Let's try this ice cream cone on for size!
I think it would be a
pretty cool horn...

No, I'm a---

That's my HORN!
I NEED that!

GIVE ME BACK MY HORN!

We're in the rhinoceros enclosure.
So of course you're a rhino.

That's right – I am!
My name's Lulu, who are you?

I'm Flom Flom. I'm a tickbird.
Every rhino has a tickbird, and every tickbird has a rhino.

PLOP!

Except for me,
that is.